W9-BED-195

Disney's
Winnie the Pooh
Give It Your All

Finishing what you begin

Will make you very proud.

You'll feel so good

When you are through

You'll shout "Hooray!" out loud!

It was the day of the "Big Race" in the Hundred-Acre Wood, and everyone was buzzing with excitement. Pooh and his friends—except Piglet—were all getting ready for the race. Piglet was a little too scared to try.

Instead, Piglet was hanging his sheets out to dry. Pooh
helped him for a little while. Suddenly a gust of wind blew
Pooh off his feet.

When the wind died down and the sheets were hung, Pooh
rushed off. "I have to get ready for the race," he said.

Piglet thanked Pooh for his help and wished his friend good luck. But after Pooh left, Piglet thought, "I really don't want to be left out of the race. Maybe I won't win, but I could give it a try!"

Now all Piglet needed was something to race in. He decided to build a little cart for himself.

He borrowed some wheels from Rabbit's old wheelbarrows.
Building his cart was easier than he'd thought.
Piglet was quite pleased with his cart until Christopher Robin rode
by on a bright red scooter.

"Rabbit told me you're entering the race, Piglet. Good for you!" shouted Christopher Robin.

"Do you like my cart?" Piglet asked.

"That's a fine cart," Christopher Robin replied. "But how will you make it go?"

Piglet hadn't thought about that.

"Maybe I shouldn't enter the race after all," he sighed.

"Don't give up, Piglet!" Christopher Robin said. "You'll think of something!"

Suddenly Tigger sprang by. "Watch out, Little Buddy! I'm bouncing through!" Tigger cried.

Before Piglet could move out of the way, Tigger bounced him into the air with a giant BOING!

"Hiya, Piglet Ol' Pal," said Tigger. "Look at my springs! Hoo-hoo! I can even bounce backwards! I'm going to use these spring-a-ma-jigs to win the race!"

"Oh, my!" thought Piglet. "Springs are the perfect idea!"

So Piglet tried adding springs to his cart, but it kept bouncing into the air and landing upside down.

"Springs may work for tiggers," Piglet said, "but they're definitely not working for me!"

Just as Piglet finished putting the wheels back on his cart,
Rabbit came hopping by on a pogo stick.

"This pogo stick is perfect!" Rabbit said aloud. "I'll get a jump
on the others and cross the finish line first."

Piglet nodded. "I wish I could use those on my cart."

"Why, there's nothing to it!" Rabbit said. "Just put pogo sticks on the corners of your cart." But Piglet didn't have any pogo sticks—especially not *four* of them.

Still, Piglet didn't lose hope. There had to be some way to make his cart go! Just then he saw Eeyore pass by, pushing Pooh in a rickety old wagon.

"Perhaps Eeyore could help me," thought Piglet.

"Oh, Eeyore, would you push my cart, too?" Piglet asked.

"Sorry, Piglet. Already got one to push," Eeyore groaned. "And it's a heavy one, too."

"How can I enter the race now?" Piglet wondered.

"I'll help you think, Piglet," Pooh offered, "if you can wait until after lunch. I don't think very well on a rumbly tummy."

"Oh, Pooh," sighed Piglet, "that will be too late."

"Well," Pooh suggested, "perhaps you could ride in my wagon."

Piglet almost said yes. But then he remembered what he'd set out to do. He had wanted to enter the race on his own.

"Thanks, Pooh," Piglet told him. "But I'll think of something. Good luck!"

As Pooh and Eeyore left, another gust of wind rushed through the trees. It blew through Piglet's sheets until they billowed up in the air. And that gave Piglet an idea.

Not far off in the meadow, the race was about to begin.
Everyone was lining up at the starting point.

"Are you ready, everybody?" Kanga called out from the
finish line.

Piglet shouted, "Wait for me!" He pushed his cart up to the
starting line, gasping for breath.

"Piglet, you're here!" Pooh cheered.

Just then, Kanga cried, "On your mark. Get set. Go!"

Tigger sprang into the lead with one bounce of his springy feet. Christopher Robin was close behind on his scooter. Rabbit, on his pogo stick, hopped into third place, followed by Pooh and Eeyore, and then little Roo on his tricycle.

But poor Piglet was still at the starting line.

"I'm not giving up yet!" Piglet thought to himself. Then he reached down to the bottom of his cart and pulled out a big white sheet. He grabbed it by the corners and lifted it into the air.

The wind filled up the sheet and began to push the cart along.
Piglet had made a sail!
In a flash, Piglet passed by Pooh and Eeyore.
"Hooray for Piglet!" Pooh cheered.

A moment later Piglet rolled by a surprised-looking Rabbit.
"Piglet moving ahead of me? Why, it's unheard of!" Rabbit thought.
Piglet swelled with pride. He was finally in the race!

Then, to his surprise, Piglet saw Tigger and Christopher
Robin in front of him. He was catching up to them!
But with every push, Christopher Robin scooted ahead.
BOING! Tigger gave a great big bounce and took the lead again.

The finish line was a few feet ahead. Tigger gave one final jump, while Christopher Robin gave one last push. But they were too late.

Piglet's cart crossed the finish line first!

"Piglet is the winner!" Kanga announced.

Piglet could hardly believe he had won!

"Now I understand," thought Piglet with a great big smile.

"I feel so proud of myself because I did what I set out to do.

I gave it my all."

A LESSON A DAY POOH'S WAY

Finish something you

set out to do,

and you'll feel as

proud as Piglet!